THE GIRL WHO WOULD
RATHER CLIMB TREES

The Girl Who Would Rath

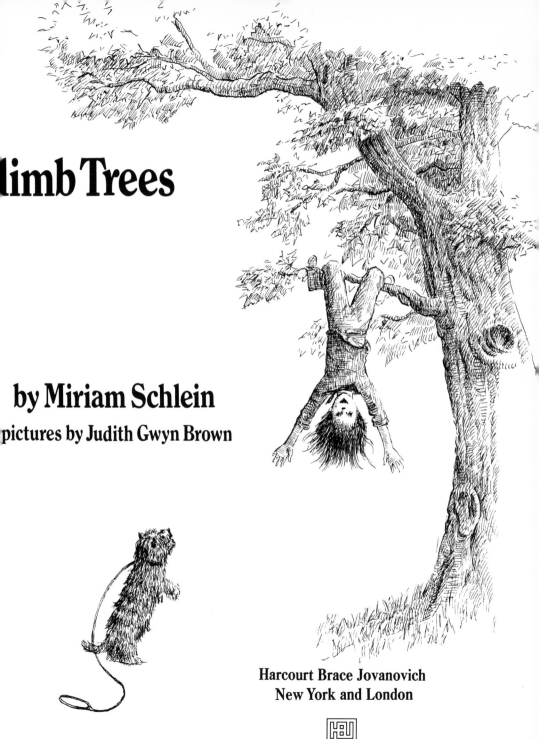

limb Trees

by Miriam Schlein
pictures by Judith Gwyn Brown

Harcourt Brace Jovanovich
New York and London

Printed in the United States of America

First edition

B C D E F G H I J K

Library of Congress Cataloging in Publication Data

Schlein, Miriam.
  The girl who would rather climb trees.

  SUMMARY: Melissa, a little girl who would rather
climb trees than play with dolls, hardly knows what to
do with the doll she is given.
  [1. Dolls—Fiction. 2. Sex role—Fiction]
I. Brown, Judith Gwyn. II. Title.
PZ7.S347Gi   [E]   75-11591
ISBN 0-15-230978-0

also by Miriam Schlein

METRIC—THE MODERN WAY TO MEASURE

This is Melissa. Melissa is a particular girl who
lives in a particular house on a particular street in
Brooklyn. But you could say, too, in a way, that
Melissa is a lot of different Melissas.

There is Melissa the bird-watcher

Melissa the roller-skater,

Melissa the cook.

here is Melissa the puzzle-doer,

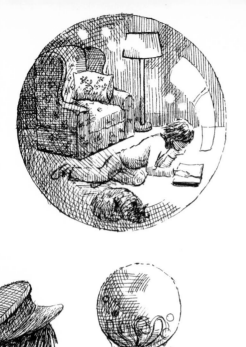

Melissa the reader,

Melissa the ballplayer,

Melissa the tree-climber.

She can do a lot of other things, too, as they come along. And she is pretty good at them. In fact, Melissa is pretty much an all-around girl.

One day there was a surprise for Melissa at home.
She walked into the kitchen and found there a large
carriage with a large doll lying in it.

"Isn't it darling?" said her mother. "It's for *you*."

"Pick it up," said her grandmother.
Melissa started to pick up the carriage.
"No, no, the doll!"
It was a fancy doll with hard pink cheeks and yellow hair and stiff legs.
"Thank you," said Melissa. "It's very nice."
She did not know quite how to hold it. She held it first like a grocery bag.

"No, no," the others shouted.
She shifted it to under her arm like a roll of carpeting.

"No, no," said her mother's best friend. *"This* way."

Melissa clutched the doll to her front. The yellow hair brushed against her nose. It made her sneeze. Melissa banged her tooth against the doll's hard cheek.

She did not know what else to *do* with the doll, so she walked around the house with it from room to room, carrying it the correct way. When she got to the living room, she laid the doll down in a big chair.

"Darling . . . sweet . . . two-of-a-kind . . ." said
her grandmother, her mother, and her mother's best
friend.

Melissa was glad that her doll made everybody happy, and she felt rather bad that it didn't make *her* feel as happy as it seemed to make everybody else feel. But after all, you couldn't throw it or catch

it or read it or race with it or even have it play with
you as you could with Snoofu the dog. And when
you carried it, you couldn't run or jump rope or
throw a ball or ride a bike or do anything *but* carry
it.

All you could do was try to pretend it was a real baby. "And," thought Melissa, "it's not like a real baby at all." It was *nothing* like her cousin Philip, who was bald and mushy-faced and soft and who ate and drooled and yelled and grabbed your finger. Philip was a lot more exciting than a doll. He was fun because you didn't know what he might do next. But you did know what a doll would do next —nothing.

"You could change her," said her grandmother.
"For what?" asked Melissa.
"I mean change her dress," said her grandmother.
"Oh, this dress is O.K.," said Melissa.

Melissa did not want to spend the whole day just sitting there, holding the doll. So she put it back into the carriage and wheeled it into her room.

Then she came tiptoeing out.
"Shhh," she said. "Dolly's asleep."

Melissa's grandmother, her mother, and her mother's best friend all smiled.

Then Melissa went
out to have some fun

and climbed three trees in a row.